Best Friends Forever

Owen Hart ♥ Judi Abbot

WALTHAM FOREST LIBRARIES

904 000 00605733

Some friends are funny . . .

. . . some friends are **wise**.

And some make you smile
with a happy surprise!

Some friends are playful,
some friends are brave.

And some melt your heart
with a warm little wave.

Some friends are **kind**
and know just what to say,

Bringing the sunshine
to brighten your day.

Friends can be found
everywhere you might go,

But there's one friend more special
than any I know . . .

Who hears all my secrets,
who shares in my fun,
Who thinks up adventures
to have in the sun.

There's simply no end
to the things we can do.
My best friend forever
will always be . . .

...you!

LITTLE TIGER PRESS
an imprint of the Little Tiger Group,
1 Coda Studios, 189 Munster Road, London SW6 6AW
www.littletiger.co.uk
First published in Great Britain 2018

Text by Owen Hart
Text copyright © Little Tiger Press 2018
Illustrations copyright © Judi Abbot 2018

Judi Abbot has asserted her right to be identified
as the illustrator of this work under the Copyright,
Designs and Patents Act, 1988.

A CIP catalogue record for this book is available from the British Library
All rights reserved
ISBN 978-1-84869-874-1
Printed in China
LTP/1400/1973/0917
2 4 6 8 10 9 7 5 3 1